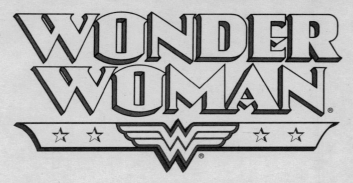

WONDER WOMAN®

The Journey Begins

Written by Nina Jaffe
Illustrated by Ben Caldwell

Wonder Woman created by
William Moulton Marston

Har
A Division of

For Bob, with love.
—N. J.

For my grandmother, artist and teacher.
—B. C.

Acknowledgments:
The author is grateful to George Pérez and Len Wein, whose
work on the Wonder Woman series provided inspiration for
this book; and to George Nicholson, for his guidance and
support throughout.
—N. J.

Wonder Woman: The Journey Begins
Copyright © 2004 DC Comics. All Rights Reserved.
Wonder Woman and all titles, characters, and related elements are trademarks of DC Comics.
HarperCollins®, ♣®, and HarperFestival® are trademarks of HarperCollins Publishers Inc.
No part of this book may be used or reproduced in any manner whatsoever without written permission
except in the case of brief quotations embodied in critical articles and reviews. Printed in the United
States of America. For information address HarperCollins Children's Books, a division of HarperCollins
Publishers, 1350 Avenue of the Americas, New York, NY 10019.
Library of Congress catalog card number: 2003109790
1 2 3 4 5 6 7 8 9 10
❖
First Edition
www.harperchildrens.com
www.dckids.com

▣ *Contents* ▣

Prologue

Far away, on the shores of Paradise Island, a young Amazon warrior was chosen to defend Mortals' World against a terrible enemy.

Years before, the Amazons had been granted immortality by the gods and goddesses of Mount Olympus. In return, this nation of women promised to guard the forces of Fear and Chaos hidden deep underneath their mountain caves.

The Amazons lived in peace and tranquility under the wise rule of their queen, Hippolyta. In time, the queen wished for a child and formed a baby girl from clay. The gods and goddesses gave the baby life and granted her special gifts and powers. The child, called Diana, grew up in the royal palace. Guided by the wisdom of the oracle and the best Amazon teachers, Princess Diana mastered sacred arts and skills, and learned how to use her powers wisely.

One day, the oracle read something terrible in her magic sphere. The forces of Fear and Chaos would soon be unleashed at the command of Ares, the god of war. Mortals' World, and everything in it, might soon be destroyed!

Only a true champion could thwart these wicked plans, and so the Amazons held a contest. Though Hippolyta wished to keep her daughter safe, Diana bravely entered the competition and won! Now it is she who is entrusted to bring the Amazons' message to Mortals' World.

Armed with her Golden Lasso of Truth, her silver bracelets, and the wisdom of her people,

Princess Diana—now known as Wonder Woman—left her home to embark on this vital mission of peace and justice.

1
The Arrival

Feeling the wind rush against her as she flew, Wonder Woman veered toward a harbor at the edge of a great city. Circling above, she could see tall buildings of stone and steel.

It was late afternoon, and as she gazed below, she saw streets filled with many people. She decided to land somewhere in the city, but away from the crowds.

Who knows how mortals will greet me? she thought to herself.

In the lowering dusk, she spotted a place that looked right—a small park.

This seems safe, she thought as she glided down gently, landing near a sturdy maple tree.

In the crisp fall air, leaves were turning red and yellow. Cold winds and leaves crackling under her feet were new sensations, and the Amazon Princess shivered slightly as she recalled the warm, sunlit mountains and valleys of Paradise Island.

The park was almost empty now. She saw some parents flinging woolen scarves around their toddlers. Boys and girls leaving the game fields were pulling hats over their ears and zipping up their jackets.

Wonder Woman looked at her own clothes. *Hmmm,* she thought. *Problem number one: How will I walk around the city without being noticed? And it wouldn't hurt to have some kind of protective garment.*

Even Amazon warriors feel the cold!

Looking around, she noticed a box with strange markings on it near a playground. Wonder Woman came closer to analyze them. On Paradise Island she had been trained to speak and read all the languages of Mortals' World.

This is definitely one of the Indo-European tongues, she said to herself. *English, in fact. The markings read* LOST AND FOUND. *If that's the case, I might borrow some clothing for myself. Maybe later I'll find the true owners. But at least with these clothes I won't stand out in a crowd!*

Helping herself to a jacket, some jeans, and a scarf, Wonder Woman set out to investigate the world of the city.

2
Rescue in the Night

As she walked through the crowds, Wonder Woman took in hundreds of new sights, sounds, and smells. Stores were lit up and neon lights flashed incessantly. On street corners, vendors were standing by carts, and strange new aromas filled the air.

Here were the citizens of Mortals' World whom she had studied and learned about. Now she was among them—women and men, young girls and boys, walking in groups, alone, or in pairs. Some walked quickly, laughing and

chattering. Others moved slowly, with care-worn expressions.

Wonder Woman heard people speaking English, but she heard other languages, too. *Back on Paradise Island, we all speak in the Greek of the ancients,* she thought to herself. *But here is another kind of music!* Soon, she found she could distinguish the lilting sounds of Spanish,

Arabic, Hindi, and Chinese.

Just then, a wailing sound pierced the night air. Wonder Woman was startled and instinctively put her hands over her ears. On her island, all the sounds she had heard were of soothing breezes, the songs of birds, or the gentle strum of harps and rhythmic drumbeats. Never had she heard such a loud, ear-shattering pitch.

What could this mean? It must be an alarm of some kind.

Quickly re-orienting herself, Wonder Woman looked around. Then she saw what must be the source: A large red truck, its lights flashing, was careening down the avenue.

Wonder Woman changed to her Amazon clothes, and with a graceful leap, sped over the traffic.

Someone must need help!

The Amazon Princess swiftly followed the truck's winding path, watching as cars pulled aside to clear the way for it as best they could. After a few twists and turns down narrow streets, the truck stopped in front of a five-story building. Flames were visible through the building windows and smoke was billowing out the front door.

"My children are still inside!" a man cried. "We live on the top floor!"

The firefighters backed up their truck close to the building, and began to set up their ladder. From her position above the building, Diana saw two small figures waving a sheet. The children had managed to climb out onto the roof!

If I wait any longer, it might be too late! Without hesitating, Wonder Woman landed on the roof, her golden tiara glinting as she ran toward the children.

"Hold on!" she said as the roof started to creak and groan. "I'll take you down!"

"Hurry!" the girl cried out. "The roof is caving in!"

Just in time, Wonder Woman used her

strong arms to lift the children high off the burning roof. She pulled them from the flames and flew. She carried them to the doorway of another building, away from the crowds.

Slowly, gently, the Amazon Princess released the boy and girl. "Your family is waiting," she said. "You can go now."

The children ran to their father. "My kids— they're safe!" he exclaimed, hugging them to his chest. "But how did you make it down so quickly?"

The children pointed excitedly to the doorway across the street. "Look, Dad! There's the woman who saved us!"

People nearby turned to look at the figure of Wonder Woman as she stood, tall and commanding, in the shadows.

The firefighters had control of the blaze now. The building would be saved, and the families who lived there would still have their homes.

Everyone cheered, and then whispered to one another in excited curiosity, "Who is she?"

"Did you see that?"

"How did she get up to the roof?"

Wonder Woman understood everything they said. But she wasn't ready to reveal her identity just yet. She had to find Ares, the god of war, and stop his plans for the destruction of Mortals' World. The less he knew of her arrival, the more time she would have to make plans of her own.

I'll have to keep everyone in mystery for a little while longer, she thought.

And so, with one last wave to the children she had rescued, Wonder Woman flew back to the park. She felt happy there, for the trees reminded her of the forest trails on Paradise Island, and the leaf-covered soil felt warm and familiar.

I'd better come up with a name for myself, she thought as she wrapped herself in the jacket and scarf. *I'll keep Diana—but I'm not a princess here. How about 'Prince?' Diana Prince. That should work.*

Slowly she fell asleep, her first day in Mortals' World behind her.

3
Assembly Hall

The next morning, traffic in the city was slower than usual. That was because an international body of representatives had gathered at the great Assembly Hall. All around the globe, people were fighting about one of Earth's most precious resources—water. One by one the representatives reported their stories.

"In our country, the people fight over who will get water from the city reservoirs!" said one.

"In our country," said another, "people are coming to blows over where the cattle will graze. They are blocking off rivers and dams. This has never happened before!"

No one was certain about the cause, but the assembly members were hoping to find a way to stop the conflicts before the violence escalated on a global scale.

In the back of the meeting hall, a tall figure dressed in a gray cape sat and watched silently.

My plan is working. Soon, I will have whole nations pitted one against the other. All of Mortals' World will worship me and me alone! No other god or goddess will have power equal to mine—Ares, god of war! Wrapping his cloak around himself, he walked silently out of the hall.

Indeed, long before this moment in time, Ares had sought to take the rule of the world away from Zeus and the gods and goddesses of Mount Olympus.

The gods knew that human beings were not yet ready to live in complete harmony. And so, in their council hall high above Mortals' World, they had decided that until people understood for themselves the true value of peace and justice, mortals would live in a condition of balance. There would be conflict but also times of calm, when people could use their human powers to create works of beauty and necessity, and share the Earth's resources.

The gods themselves had learned to live in peace only after long years of terrible wars—for in the beginning of time, Chronos, father of the gods and goddesses, grew jealous and tried to destroy his children. It was then that Zeus, his son, rose up against Chronos and

conquered him, banishing his father to the dark caves of the netherworld.

Then Zeus, with the help of his children— Athena, goddess of wisdom; Artemis, goddess of the moon; Aphrodite, goddess of love; and Hermes, the messenger—established the Council of Peace.

Soon other immortals joined its ranks, and it was by the consent of this council that Zeus reigned on Mount Olympus. The gods and goddesses knew that if he were ever to break the rule of peace in their world, his reign would come to an end and another would be there to take his place.

But Ares, the god of war, had never accepted the council or Zeus's status as their

supreme ruler. Born at the time of the wars with Chronos, Ares reveled in violence and disruption, and drew energy from the conflicts on Earth. From his mountain fortress called Areopagus, he plotted year after year, century after century. There he built up the forces of his armies and waited for his chance to strike and conquer.

The wars of Mortals' World gave him strength, yet this was not enough. In his insatiable lust for power, Ares would only be happy with complete domination. The balance, he felt, must finally be tipped in his favor! And so, with great secrecy, he sent out scores of his warlings, disguised as mortals, to stir up trouble and cause conflict.

In their disguises, he thought, *my warlings won't be discovered by the Olympians until it's too late!*

4
A World in Turmoil

That morning, Wonder Woman left her refuge in the park and walked back to the city streets. She saw small crowds huddled next to their radios and others gathered around newsstands.

I wonder if this is something unusual? she thought. *Maybe I can learn more about it.*

Wonder Woman saw people exchanging paper bills or coins for the newspapers. Since she had no money of her own, at least for now, she joined one of the groups at a radio, hoping

to gather whatever information she could.

As she leaned in, Wonder Woman listened to the radio announcer report, "Representatives from around the globe are meeting in Assembly Hall as people of the world battle over water rights. . . ."

Wonder Woman shook her head. *This is what the oracle foretold! Ares's plan is already set in motion.*

Somehow he is destroying the ability of mortals to reason with one another. It's up to me to do something about it!

Wonder Woman remembered one of the sayings she had learned from the wise oracle back home. "Only with knowledge can true change take place."

The Amazon Princess decided to leave the city and find out what was happening with her own eyes.

Swiftly she flew from country to country and from continent to continent. Everywhere she went, she could see the same thing. In every region, people were taunting one another, claiming water rights for their own. In the farmlands, people were building walls around the irrigation pipes and blocking off streams. In the cities, people set up their own guards around the fountains and reservoirs. Neighbors were pitted against neighbors, and sometimes they came to blows.

But how did all of these conflicts start? If only she could find the source!

5
Sent from Areopagus

Wonder Woman decided to locate a town that was still peaceful. After searching, she finally found one hidden in a valley. Once she landed, she looked for the nearest stream and waited, hidden by the branches of a tall pine tree.

At daybreak, two farmhands came to collect water. Before they could dip their buckets, a figure appeared. He was dressed no differently than anyone else, but Wonder Woman saw that underneath his jacket he wore a vest of chain mail, and his eyes glowed like red fire.

"Do you think there is really enough water for both your farms?" he whispered in one man's ear. "Don't you know he's trying to take over the stream for himself? You'd better do something, before it's too late!"

The farm worker scratched his head. He had always shared the water. As he listened, though, his eyes glazed over. Then he turned to his companion, and spoke in a loud, monotone voice, "What are you doing here? This is *my* stream! There's only enough water here for one of us!"

The second farmhand dropped his bucket in surprise. "What's gotten into you, friend?" he asked.

Without answering, the farmhand picked up his neighbor's bucket and hurled it across the stream. "That's all the water you'll be taking

back to your fields, today or any day!" Before long, the two men were caught in a wrestling match, each one trying to throw the other to the ground.

The figure with glowing eyes chuckled to himself and slowly backed away. "Ah," she

heard him whisper. "Soon the whole valley will be in an uproar. I must return to Areopagus and report back to my commander—one more town is now under his control!"

The Amazon Princess realized this was her

chance. If she could find Ares and confront him, maybe she could stop him before the conflict spread any further. Leaping in front of the agent, Wonder Woman stood, sword and shield in hand, looking into his eyes as she spoke, "So, servant of Ares, are you pleased with your work today?"

The warling was stunned. Who was this young woman with the glittering tiara and long, dark hair? No one had ever tried to stop him before!

"I don't know who you are, or who sent you, but get out of my way!" The warling growled and tried to push past her, but Wonder Woman blocked him easily. With one quick step, she threw the creature off balance and pinned him to the ground with her sword.

"You may be able to hide from the innocent people of Mortals' World," she said, "but not from the women of Paradise Island!"

The servant scrambled to his feet and started to run. Ahead of them was a canyon with small dark caves cut into the mountainside. If he reached one, he could hide in its dark tunnels. Wonder Woman knew she would never be able to find him there. But before the warling reached the rocky slopes, she sped even faster and blocked his way.

"Now, coward, know that I am Wonder Woman—daughter of the Amazon queen Hippolyta. I have been sent by my people to turn Ares from his path of destruction! If you wish to see Areopagus again, tell me—where can I find him?"

Wonder Woman didn't have long to wait. Before her captive had time to answer, a swirling mist emerged from within the caves. It grew larger, spinning outward with the ferocity of a whirlwind, until from out of its fiery clouds stood Ares, the god of war himself!

6
Ares, the God of War

Wonder Woman had heard of Ares ever since she was a small child. She knew of his warlike ways, and of his eternal hatred for the Olympians and their dream of peace for Mortals' World. Yet she had never encountered him in his full incarnation. His metal armor clanked and groaned, and the earth shook under the weight of his heavy spear. His eyes glowed a fiery red.

"Could it be?" he thundered. "Have the Amazons really dared to send their warrior sister to come after the great Ares?"

Wonder Woman stepped back. Then she took a deep breath and began to speak. "Ares, why do you try your powers in this foolish way? Do you really think you can overpower the Olympians? Mortals' World has its own destiny. You cannot bend the people of Earth to your will!"

Ares grimaced as he spoke. "Amazon pretender, how little you know! My dominion was prophesized long ago—for when Zeus used force to overthrow Chronos, he created the thirst for violence in his precious dimension of mortals. I have only shaped their weak will to fit *my* needs. And now I have come to claim my prize! It is time for the rule of Zeus and the Olympians to end!"

Wonder Woman stood her ground. She felt fear, but her determination was even stronger. "Don't you know that the Amazons were called upon by the gods and goddesses to protect this world from the likes of you? This is the very reason the Olympians granted me powers. Why do you hide behind your servants and send them to do your bidding? Are you afraid to face me on your own?"

"You do me an injustice, Amazon," Ares answered in a low voice. "The path of destruction that lies ahead is far too powerful, even for an Amazon warrior!" And with that he lashed out, hurling a spear at Wonder Woman.

Quickly the Amazon Princess raised her arms in defense, deflecting the spear with her silver bracelets. As Ares threw spear after spear, again and again, she warded off his blows with ease.

"So you think those silver bracelets of yours will protect you? Just remember, long ago

those bracelets were part of the chains that enslaved your mother and sisters! Soon you will all be in chains again!"

Diana stepped back. "Ares, you will never defeat me," she called out, reaching for her sword and shield.

But Ares didn't wait. In a blinding explosion of light, he hurled Wonder Woman beyond the confines of Mortals' World into the depths of his mountain fortress. Between its cold walls,

Wonder Woman was held in utter darkness—a void where not even the light of the stars could penetrate. "Now, Wonder Woman, you will see the fulfillment of *my* destiny."

A swirling mist appeared before her again. This time, as she gazed into its depths, she saw Mortals' World—crumbled and decayed. Only the servants of Ares inhabited its shores and deserts. Mortals, exhausted by war and conflict, were forced to live in slavery, obeying the commands of the god of war and his minions. Homes and farmlands, cities and bridges, halls of art and science—all lay in ruins as despair reigned. Tears came to her eyes as Wonder Woman gazed in horror. "Athena protect us!"

Ares shook his head. "Your goddesses cannot help you. Nor can Zeus. Not even your Amazon sisters!"

As Wonder Woman gazed further into the mist, she saw the truth of his words. Paradise Island itself was fading to oblivion. Queen Hippolyta and her people were about to cross the river of the netherworld, never to appear again in the realms of mortals or gods. Their strength was weakening; their palace walls were turning to dust.

"What shall we do?" the queen whispered in a hoarse voice. "Is it really time to lead my people to the domain of Hades?"

But the oracle comforted her. "Never, my queen—for as long as Diana lives, there is hope for us all. Remember, it was your love and wish for a new life on Paradise Island that created her—and that is stronger than even the gifts of the gods! Send her that love now. It is the only weapon she has left!"

7
The Lasso of Truth

Dazed by the overwhelming power of Ares's dark prophecy, Wonder Woman knelt in sorrow. *How can I combat his terrible onslaught?* she wondered. *Can I save Mortals' World and my own people from the devastation?*

The glow of her silver bracelets was dimmed. Her sword could not help her, and her shield offered no protection. As she contemplated the answer, she felt a warm light enter her heart. As if in a dream, a spirit of love and compassion had penetrated the walls of

Ares's mighty fortress, giving her hope and strength. Wonder Woman remembered the gentle sunlight of Paradise Island and the wise words of the oracle. "In times of great fear and darkness, always look within and remember who you are. The light of truth will guide you."

Slowly, hesitating at first, she rose once more to her feet, concentrating her thoughts. *Maybe I can't overpower Ares by might*, she realized, *but I can* show *him where his own plans would lead!*

In the dark shadows, Wonder Woman reached for the gleaming weapon she carried at her side: the great Golden Lasso of Truth, forged by the god Hephaestus from the adornments of Gaea, goddess of the earth, and tempered with the embers of eternal truth. Now it was her turn to show Ares a vision.

"Foolish Amazon!" the war god laughed as he saw her rise. "It's too late—your magic lasso cannot help you now!"

Ignoring his words, Wonder Woman flung the golden rope around the towering figure of Ares. Like the coils of a shining serpent, the

lasso encircled him ever more tightly.

"You cannot destroy me, for that would be the end of your own powers!" cried Ares. "The path of destruction is not in your destiny!"

As she stood beside him, Wonder Woman looked at him, half in pity, then spoke in a slow, measured voice. "Ares, I've not come to destroy you—but to *teach* you. Look now at the vision that only the Lasso of Truth can bestow. Look well and decide for yourself."

Trapped in its coils, Ares had no choice but to obey. As he gazed through a golden aura cast by the lasso, he witnessed the final stages of his plan for domination. In the ravaged landscape, smoke and ash rose from every corner of the globe. There were no mortals left. Even his own armies had disappeared, for they no longer had purpose. Ares was truly the master of Mortals' World, but he was alone.

Finally, even he would fade into oblivion, joining the Olympians he had banished to the never-ending shadows of the netherworld.

Enmeshed in the Golden Lasso of Truth, Ares saw for the first time the inevitable consequences of his plan. For without mortals, his own powers would wane. In the end even his name would be forgotten—unknown, unmourned—stricken from the farthest

reaches of the universe.

Ares shook his head. "No, it cannot be! My dreams of glory all lead to this?"

Wonder Woman called out, her spirit of compassion shining through her anger. "It is the *truth*, mighty Ares. For your own sake, for the sake of the Olympians, and for the ever-turning generations of Mortals' World—you must stop the cycle of violence before it is too late!"

Feeling her powers begin to return, the Amazon Princess then released the god of war from her lasso.

8
Victory, for Now

Ares was stunned by the vision Wonder Woman had revealed. He sent a message to his forces to undo the spells of hatred they had cast throughout Mortals' World, and return to Areopagus. He needed time to regain his confidence and think.

One by one, in the towns and villages, cities and suburbs, people took down the barriers they had created and returned to sharing water from their reservoirs, lakes, and streams. Even in places where there were no easy solutions, people began peaceful discussions to solve their disagreements.

"Ares, you will not regret this. In time you, too, may be turned from the prophecy of Chronos and find a new path to Olympian glory."

"Amazon, I hereby release you from the dungeons of Areopagus. For now, you have my word—I will no longer attempt to bend Mortals' World to my will. The threat of unending violence is over, and the condition of balance restored. But remember—their fascination with war is what gives me strength!"

"There is no limit to the potential for good among mortals," Wonder Woman replied with a smile. "The Olympians have given me the wisdom and the power to help them discover and harness this for themselves."

In a flash, Ares released Wonder Woman

from the confines of his fortress walls. Once
again, she found herself in the valley where
she had first met him face to face. The fiery
mists had faded, but his mocking voice echoed
in her ears.

"It will not be an easy task, Amazon—we shall see if you are equal to it! If you are not, then beware, for the world shall hear from me again!"

9
Return to the City

Wonder Woman picked up her golden lasso. She wound it carefully, and fastened it to her belt. She brushed the dust off her silver bracelets, returned her sword to its sheath, and picked up her shield. Then she offered up a prayer to the gods and goddesses of Mount Olympus. She was sure they had been watching over her as she had fought for the survival of Mortals' World.

"Oh, Athena, goddess of wisdom, thank you for giving my words strength and power.

Thank you, Artemis, goddess of the hunt, for giving me speed and quickness. And thank you, Hestia, goddess of the hearth, for giving my heart the warmth and compassion to outlast fear and anger. I am an Amazon, and ours is the way of peace."

Wonder Woman sent love and appreciation to her mother, the queen, to the oracle, and to her Amazon sisters. She knew it was their faith and caring that had entered her heart, giving her strength as she was trapped in the walls of Areopagus.

On Paradise Island, Hippolyta and the oracle smiled at one another. Diana had met Ares's challenge with courage and wisdom. The Amazons and their way of life would continue, just as the Olympians had decreed.

As Wonder Woman flew back over the mountains and valleys, she could see, even from a distance, that things were returning to the way they were, as people began to rebuild their lives.

When she reached the city where she had first landed, the Amazon Princess returned to the park and found where she had stashed her clothes. Dressed like any young woman on a city street, Wonder Woman made her way to Assembly Hall, where all the representatives were gathered together once again. This time, they were smiling and shaking hands.

"We're not sure how it happened," they were saying to one another, "but somehow our people have begun to cooperate."

"The fighting over water rights has subsided considerably," one ambassador said.

"Yes, we hope this won't be just a passing phase," said another, "for we still have much work to do if today's children are going to have everything they need to live long and happy lives."

The representatives had good news to take back home. "Maybe now," they said, "we can attend to the other important things, like making sure each and every family in the world has a place to live and enough food to eat!"

Diana listened. She knew not every problem could be solved at once, but at least she had helped to pave the way.

Just then a reporter came up to her. "You look like you're new in town. Do you have any opinion on this recent turn of events?"

Diana smiled. "I'm just glad to hear words of hope coming from our leaders. I trust this is the beginning of a new era for the world."

"Can I quote you on that?" the reporter asked. "What's your name?"

Diana hesitated a moment. "My name? It's Diana. Diana Prince."

The reporter jotted it down and then looked up to ask another question, but she was gone.

Diana walked quickly through the streets. Things were better now, but she remembered the challenge of Ares. How long would this peace last? And what about all the other problems she'd heard about at Assembly Hall? Diana longed to go home to the gardens and flowing streams of Paradise Island. She missed

her friends and her time meandering on forest trails. She missed her mother and the calm, wise voice of the temple oracle. But Wonder Woman knew her task was far from over. Her mission was to bring a message of peace and justice to Mortals' World. Her journey had only just begun.

The Amazon Credo

Mortals have corrupted many of the laws set before us. Therefore, our nation of women warriors is dedicated to the ideal of uniting all people as one.

No longer will violence and greed rule, for now we Amazons have been called upon to temper aggression with compassion, lend reason to rage, and overcome hatred with love.

We are a nation of women dedicated to our sisters, to our beliefs, and to the peace that is humankind's right.

We are Amazons, and we have come to save Mortals' World.